# Orangutan Who Sang

Jay Vincent

Stew Wright

Written for Olly and any
little monkeys who have
ever felt scared or shy.
It will all be ok, I promise.

It can be so hard for us to speak to the tiny people in our lives sometimes,
especially about those matters which may be troubling them. Whether it's
shyness, lack of confidence or loneliness, we hope that books like this will help us
bigger people have those difficult conversations at the right time and help our
children make sense of their feelings and start to understand them.

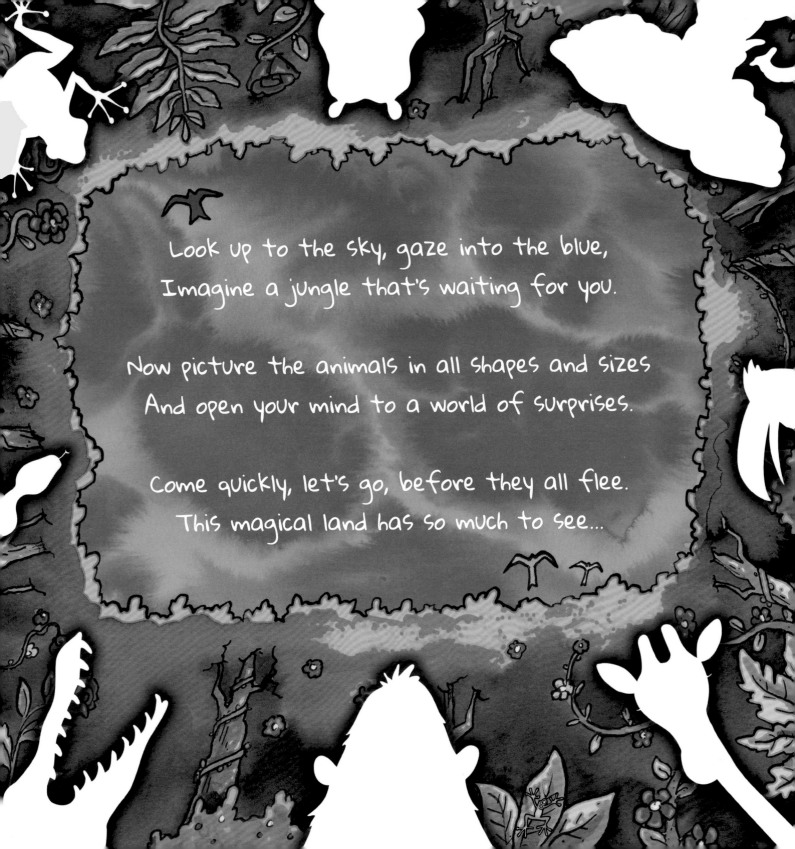

Look up to the sky, gaze into the blue,
Imagine a jungle that's waiting for you.

Now picture the animals in all shapes and sizes
And open your mind to a world of surprises.

Come quickly, let's go, before they all flee.
This magical land has so much to see...

What's that over there? A big jungle school
Full of animals playing... isn't it cool?

There are baby crocs and stripy adders
Playing with rocks and snakes and ladders.

There's the tiniest frog you'll ever have seen
Bouncing around on a huge trampoline.

And can you spot the toucans with big yellow beaks?
They spend all their time playing hide and go seek!

But wait, who's that creature way up in the trees?
Above the giraffes, the birds and the bees?
Why it's Olly the Orangutan! (He's kind of a monkey)
He's orange and hairy and really quite funky.

But Olly is different from most girls and boys,
Not playing with Poohsticks, not playing with toys.

For he has a talent, an incredible voice,
He'd sing night and day if he had the choice.

But you won't hear him sing, not this hairy guy.
Although Olly's big, he's incredibly shy.

The whole problem started a long time ago
When Olly attended the school talent show.

He thought he was ready, his mouth open wide
But the sounds were all silent, whatever he tried.

He's struggled so often to quash all these fears
But whenever he tries, it just ends up in tears.
So that's where we find him, up high in the sky,
All on his own, a solitary guy.

But hold on a second, isn't he big?
Too big to be sitting on that flimsy twig?
It's starting to bend, it's starting to break.
That twig won't hold Olly and all of his weight.

"SNAP!" And with that his face turned quite pale,
Followed quite quickly by a loud monkey wail.

"Oh no!" cried a toad with a deafening croak.
"The branch that held Olly has finally broke!"

The animals gawped as he crashed to the ground,
smacking the floor with a deafening sound.
And there Olly lay for many a while,
A rough mound of fur all laid in a pile.

His friends, they were worried, so called for a nurse
But he took their concern for giggles or worse.
Seeking safety ahead, he jumped to his feet.
"He's running away!" squawked a small parakeet.

All was a blur as he rushed through the trees,
Plants, bushes and flowers all buzzing with bees.

Feeling exhausted, he searched for some shade
And found himself standing in a wild jungle glade.

Meanwhile up above our poor monkey's head,
An owl had just yawned and got out of bed.

"What's all this noise outside of my house?"
(He was hungry for lunch, and fancied a mouse).

But before he could swoop from his perch down to see
If it was a creature to have for his tea.
His ears, they were met with a marvellous sound
Floating up from beneath him, way down on the ground.

Olly was singing a beautiful song,
A hypnotic tale called 'I want to belong'.
The owl swooped and swooned to the wonderful rhyme.
His wings just like jungle drums, beating in time.

"What a tune!" screeched the owl, laughing and cheering
As he flew further down to the small open clearing.
"The places I've flown and the things that I've seen...
I never have heard a song so serene!"

But Olly was frightened, fearing the worst.
This most pensive of primates was convinced he was cursed.
As quick as he'd come, the orangutan fled
And the welcoming owl returned to his bed.

Now back at the school the creatures stood 'round,
Frightened their friend would never be found.

"Ok, listen up!" said the Gorilla Headmaster.
"If we all work together, we'll find Olly faster.

"I want you to search every tree, cave and lake.
Ask every warthog, dart frog and snake.

Now all of you go but remain in plain sight,
Especially those with the power of flight."

Not far from his friends, Olly came to a rest,
Sat by a river, heart pounding his chest.
Sitting and wondering what others had said,
"I know!" he thought. "A song might clear my head!"

Out of the river rose a pair of big eyes,
They were using the reeds as a clever disguise.
The largest of crocs was sat waiting for lunch,
Hoping for something that had a good crunch!

Yet right at that moment, Olly started to rhyme,
Was this his last action before the croc's crime?
Dreaming of nibbling a fine monkey toe,
The sound made croc stop and she swayed to and fro!

Now you'll have to wait a very long while
'Til you come across a jive crocodile!
But that's what was happening to this crazy croc,
She was out of the water and ready to rock.

Now back at the clearing without the furore,
Owl told the head ape an incredible story.
"Olly Orangutan?" said the gorilla, confused,
"I've never heard sing." He sounded bemused.

But Owl was insistent, he wanted to go
"There's no time to waste," he said, tapping his toe.
The owl flew off first with the others behind
They shouted out loud: "We've a monkey to find!"

Way out in the jungle, Olly tried not to cry,
"The croc almost ate me and I don't know why."
But then he heard something, laughter or clapping?
Or was it mischievous monkeys all rapping?

As he crept closer he started to hum.
He wanted to know where the noise had come from.
Dancing and singing and laughter and more,
All 'round a campfire ablaze on the floor.

He laughed at them all break dancing and singing,
While some banged their drums, some had bells they were ringing.

"Finally, monkeys that I can call friends,
My solitary life can come to an end."

But then Olly realised that something was odd
With this new chimp crew, his singing ape squad.

Where are these animals' tails and their claws?
Soft furry noses and warm padded paws?

"They're humans, not monkeys! Oh golly, oh jeez!"
Our monkey then smiled, and dropped to his knees.

For Olly was now no longer in doubt,
It was finally time for his rhymes to come out.

Our orange orangutan called out to the group:
"Do you mind if I join in your musical troupe?"

The scouts gathered 'round our happy ape friend
And Olly sang songs he'd previously penned.

Then all of a sudden with tunes on the breeze,
The Gorilla Headmaster emerged from the trees.

"Quick, quick everybody, just look who we've found,
I can't believe Olly was making that sound!"

And all the school animals then came into view,
As soon as he saw them, well Olly just knew...

That singing and rhyming could make his friends grin,
It was time for the group to come and join in.

The chimps they were bouncing and making a scene,
Jumping and leaping, they smashed tambourines.

The Gorilla Headmaster! Well he clearly knows
How to get the best sound from a set of bongos.

The earth it vibrated and started to quake,
Well that's what you get from a drum-playing snake.

The children and animals sang all through the night,
To Olly's excitement, joy and delight.

So farewell young Olly, go sing with your gang,
We're proud to have met you... the orangutan who sang!

# Explore the Jungle!

## Can you answer the Gorilla Headmaster's questions?

1. Can you name the eight animal silhouettes on the first page?

2. Why do you think Olly is sat on a branch all on his own?

3. Where is the cool monkey in sunglasses hiding?

4. What does the total number of ladybird's spots add up to?

5. How many toucans can you see around the jungle school?

6. Name the one animal that wears pink shorts?

7. What two colours are on the Gorilla Headmaster's tie?

8. Why does the crocodile decide not to eat Olly?

9. Why is Olly drawn to the group of scouts?

10. What instrument is the butterfly playing?

11. How many tiny frogs (like this one) are hidden throughout the book?

12. How do you think Olly feels at the end of the story?

The Orangutan Who Sang

©2019 Jay Vincent & Stew Wright

First edition printed in 2019 in the UK

ISBN: 978-1-910863-57-2

Written by: Jay Vincent

Illustrated by: Stew Wright
(www.2wrightdesign.com)

Edited by: Phil Turner, Katie Fisher

Layout by: Paul Cocker, Matt Crowder

Contributors: Ruth Alexander,
Rupinder Casimir, Lydia Fitzsimons,
Michael Johnson, Sarah Koriba,
Marek Nowicki, Sophie Westgate

Published by Mini Meze

An imprint of Meze Publishing Limited

Unit 1B, 2 Kelham Square

Kelham Riverside

Sheffield S3 8SD

Web: www.mezepublishing.co.uk

Telephone: 0114 275 7709

Email: mini@mezepublishing.co.uk